WELCOME TO
PASSPORT TO READING
A beginning reader's ticket to a brand-new world!

Every book in this program is designed to build read-along and read-alone skills, level by level, through engaging and enriching stories. As the reader turns each page, he or she will become more confident with new vocabulary, sight words, and comprehension.

These PASSPORT TO READING levels will help you choose the perfect book for every reader.

READING TOGETHER
Read short words in simple sentence structures together to begin a reader's journey.

READING OUT LOUD
Encourage developing readers to sound out words in more complex stories with simple vocabulary.

READING INDEPENDENTLY
Newly independent readers gain confidence reading more complex sentences with higher word counts.

READY TO READ MORE
Readers prepare for chapter books with fewer illustrations and longer paragraphs.

This book features sight words from the educator-supported Dolch Sight Words List. This encourages the reader to recognize commonly used vocabulary words, increasing reading speed and fluency.

For more information, please visit passporttoreadingbooks.com.

Enjoy the journey!

Little, Brown and Company
Hachette Book Group
1290 Avenue of the Americas, New York, NY 10104
Visit us at LBYR.com
mylittlepony.com

First Edition: January 2020

Little, Brown and Company is a division of Hachette Book Group, Inc. The Little, Brown name and logo are trademarks of Hachette Book Group, Inc.

The publisher is not responsible for websites (or their content) that are not owned by the publisher.

Library of Congress Control Number 2019945566

ISBNs: 978-0-316-48705-4 (pbk.), 978-0-316-48704-7 (ebook), 978-0-316-48701-6 (ebook), 978-0-316-48706-1 (ebook)

Printed in China

APS

10 9 8 7 6 5 4 3 2 1

Passport to Reading titles are leveled by independent reviewers applying the standards developed by Irene Fountas and Gay Su Pinnell in *Matching Books to Readers: Using Leveled Books in Guided Reading*, Heinemann, 1999.

Licensed By:

Fluttershy's Bunny Haven

Adapted by Rory Keane

Based on the episode "Fluttershy Leans In"

Written by Gillian M. Berrow

LITTLE, BROWN AND COMPANY

New York   Boston

Attention, My Little Pony fans!
Look for these words when you read this book. Can you spot them all?

obstacle

clinic

sanctuary

hammock

Fluttershy's pet bunny, Angel, hops through an obstacle course. He wants to win the Ponyville pet contest!

"Be careful," Fluttershy tells him.

It is too late!
Angel falls and
hurts his foot!

Fluttershy does not
have bunny foot braces.
She cannot help Angel
by herself.

Fluttershy takes her
bunny to see Dr. Fauna.
Dr. Fauna is the best
veterinarian in Equestria.

Dr. Fauna is very busy.
There are too many
animals at her clinic!

The animals are happy at the
clinic and do not want to leave.

"I know how to make the critters
happy and give you more space!"
Fluttershy says.

Fluttershy wants to build
an animal sanctuary.

A sanctuary is a safe place
where creatures can live.
Animals can move there after
Dr. Fauna makes them feel better.

Fluttershy's friends know
who can help!
Pinkie Pie says Hard Hat
can build the sanctuary.

Rarity says Dandy Grandeur
can decorate it.
Applejack says Wrangler can
create a space for each animal.

Fluttershy is excited.

She has so many ideas!

Working with these
expert ponies will be fun.

Hard Hat asks Fluttershy how
the sanctuary should look.

"The sanctuary should not have
walls," Fluttershy tells him.
"That way animals can go back
to the forest when they are ready."

Hard Hat tells Fluttershy
that he understands.
But he thinks his
ideas will be better.

"She will thank us when
she sees the sanctuary,"
he tells his team.

Dandy thinks the sanctuary should be decorated with bright colors.

"Animals will love brown
and green pillows.
Those are the colors of nature!"
Fluttershy says.

Dandy thinks he can
change Fluttershy's mind.
"Sometimes ponies do
not know what they
want!" he says.

Wrangler needs to know where
the animals should stay.

"We do not need cages,"
Fluttershy tells her.
"Animals should be
free to come and go."

Wrangler disagrees.
She thinks cages will
keep the animals safe.

Later, Fluttershy checks
on everypony's work.
Nopony listened to her!

Hard Hat is building walls!

Dandy is hanging
colorful curtains!

Wrangler is
preparing cages!

"Do you love
it?" they ask.

"I do not love it!" Fluttershy replies.
Hard Hat's doors are too small
for giraffes.

Dandy's curtains block out sunlight.
Wrangler's cages are not cozy.

"You all worked hard," Fluttershy says,
"but you did not do what I asked."
She tells the ponies she does
not need their help anymore.

Just then, Dr. Fauna
arrives with the animals.

The animals are so excited
about their new home.
They run toward it.

CRASH!

Oh no!

The animals accidentally
wreck everypony's hard work.
The sanctuary is ruined!

Fluttershy is sad, but
she does not give up!

She loves helping animals.
She will find a way to
make her dream come true.

Fluttershy starts over.
This time the sanctuary will
be built the way she wants.

Fluttershy's friends help.

Pinkie Pie builds a rope swing.

Rarity hangs a hammock.

Applejack plants some flowers.

Soon it is time to show Dr. Fauna.
"Welcome to Sweet Feather Sanctuary!"
Fluttershy says.

It is perfect!
The animals and
Dr. Fauna all love it.

It took a lot of work, but
Fluttershy is so proud of
making her dream come true!

Angel and his friends
are happy to have a big,
safe space to hop and play.